Murder Me Always

by Lee Mueller

Murder Me Always
©1995
©2010 (revised)

Characters

<u>Director</u> - is the director of the "fake"* play

<u>Wanda Hawthorne</u> - the Femme Fatale character of the "fake" play

<u>Fritz Fontaine</u>- a pompous actor who must have his way.

<u>Henry</u>- older actor a bumbling forgetful type.

<u>Trixie</u>- the assistant director who is in reality a policewoman.

<u>Muffy</u>- a spoiled rich girl

<u>Blake</u>- the male version of Muffy in some aspects but a little more devious and shady.

<u>Detective Joe Mamet-</u> a detective who has read too many 1940's detective novels

<u>Drew Graham</u>- got into acting because he couldn't find a rock band to let him join.

<u>Dolores</u>- somewhat of the typical plain Jane -librarian type.

<u>Cab Driver</u>- typical cab driver.

*fake play meaning The play the actors are trying to Present

(Director enters stage followed by Wanda and Trixie)

DIRECTOR: *(continuing from argument started off stage)* ...I don't care! All these people are here and they've paid good money!

WANDA: Most of the actors are here too! I'm ready!

TRIXIE: But should we start without him?

DIRECTOR: Look! It's very important that this play goes on tonight! Do you understand? I'm not arguing anymore! Wanda, go tell everyone to get ready. Trixie, see if you can track down our missing link! Call him, text him, skype him, friend him on Facebook, whatever you have to do!

(Trixie exits)

WANDA: *(as she exits)* Fritz isn't going to be happy!

DIRECTOR: *(rising in intensity)* Well tell Fritz to put on a shiny happy face and get it in gear. *I'm* the director! What I say, is what goes! Let's get this show on the road people! If anyone has a problem with it... well... then they'll have a problem with it! I'm not here to pamper a bunch sensitive artists! This ain't no party! This ain't no disco! I'm not fooling around! If anyone wants to question my judgment, well you can just ...*(turns to audience, dramatic change in tone -to a sugary sweet delivery)* Hi! How are you? Good! I'd like to welcome you to -----'s production of "Murder Me Always". We will start the play as soon as a small.. "issue" gets solved. *(looks off stage occasionally)* Yes, well, let me take this opportunity to explain a few things. Some of you may have seen "Murder Mysteries" and know how they work.

1

(FRITZ *appears in the wings Stage Right trying to get director's attention*)

DIRECTOR: And some may not, so let me just take a second while we're waiting and explain a few things.

(*Fritz clears throat*)

DIRECTOR: (*seeing him*) Oh look! It's Mr. Fontaine, one of the actors! Say! Maybe he would like to come out here and explain it to you. What do you say Fritz? Would you like to help your Director out of a slight jam?

FRITZ: No, actually, I wanted to..

DIRECTOR: GET OUT HERE FONTAINE AND HELP THE DIRECTOR!!

FRITZ: Yea, well..O.K. (*moves out of wings and crosses to the Director*)

DIRECTOR: Ladies and gentlemen, Mr. Fontaine will explain it all for you. (*threateningly to Fritz*) Make it snappy Monkey boy cause we're startin' this puppy whether you like it or not! (*director quickly exits*)

FRITZ: (*nervous laugh*) Well, very good. Excellent. Yes, where were we? Ah! For those of you who are new to this genre, i.e. Murder Mysteries, allow me to explain. Instead of thinking of yourselves as an "audience", imagine instead, you are all "guests" at a dinner party. You were all invited here this evening by the wealthy banker, Mr. Swanwallow. I will be playing the part or *dramatis personae* of Mr. Swanwallow this evening.

(*Wanda enters Stage right, trying to get Fritz's attention.*)

FRITZ: Now, I'll also ask you to imagine that I have invited all of you here to celebrate the lovely Birthday of our dear guest of honor, the delightful Widow Vanderventer. You dear audience, shall portray the guests!

(*Wanda clears her throat loudly*)

FRITZ: However, not all of the guests in attendance this evening were invited! In fact, some may have other agendas. They may be quite erroneous and dare I say, suspicious! Yes, and of course...

(*Wanda clears throat again.*)

FRITZ: (*noticing her*) Oh! Wanda! Uh..I mean, *Miss Sinlace*! Is everything all right? Has our "late friend" made it to our soiree?

WANDA: No, he hasn't made it and I doubt he's *sorry.*

FRITZ: Sorry? Oh no, I said *soiree*..you know.. party.

WANDA: Party? Oh! You mean *the play*! I get it. You're trying to be all in character!

FRITZ: Yes, Miss Sinlace, what was your first clue?

WANDA: Whatever Fritz or Swanwallow or whoever you are at this minute. Anyway, he sent a text that he should be here at the.. swar-ay...thing soon.

FRITZ: Splendid! Very Good!

WANDA: And the director..of the uh..swar-ay, wanted me to tell you to "*wrap it up*", cause we're going to start on time. And she's not swar-ee.

FRITZ: Yes, very cute. But actually, I think we should wait, Miss Sinlace, until everyone has arrived.

WANDA: That's cool but, you're not the director.

FRITZ: No, but I should have been! Tell you what, I shall go and *confer* with the director while you entertain our dinner guests!

WANDA: Me? No! Really, Swans you're doing a super awesome job here and..

FRITZ: Please, by all means! Ladies and gentlemen, may I present the very lovely and talented, Miss Wanda Hawthorne! (*pulls her to center*) Let's give her a hand! (*encourage applause*) Wanda will be portraying the role of Sally Sinlace this evening. Wanda, I mean... "Sally", would you be so kind as to explain to our guests, how the "mystery" will work this evening? Thank you. Excuse me. (*exits quickly*)

WANDA: (*starts after him*) Wait! Fritz!! (*reluctantly comes back to center*) Uh..Hi! How's it going? Good, good. Let's see..

(*Offstage we can hear Fritz shouting - fades down*)

WANDA: So, how this mystery works... well, tonight somebody will get killed and.. you figure it out. That's pretty much the deal. Kinda like an episode.. you know.. of CSI. Well, not CSI, because they cut people up and junk. Tonight will be like... some other show, where they don't

4

cut people up. Anyway, at the end of the play or dinner..or whatever, you'll vote and write down the name of the person you think committed the murder. Is everybody cool with that?

HENRY: (*entering as if play has started*) Night has fallen upon the day! The larks sing from the brown branches of the mighty oaks which stand tall upon these grounds outside!

WANDA: Henry!! Henry wait! Not yet!

HENRY: What a delightful evening to..Uh..what are you doing here? (*digs for script*) What scene is this?!

WANDA: We're not in any "scene" Henry! We haven't started!

HENRY: But I heard my cue! I thought I was suppose to enter after the uh..thing happens...

WANDA: The thing didn't happen! The party hasn't started!

HENRY: Party? What party?

WANDA: The sorry party! You know! The thing we're doing?

(*Fritz's offstage shouting can be heard again. Immediately he enters followed by director. The two conversations should happen at same time. Fritz talking to Director and Henry with Wanda.*)

HENRY: I thought there was a performance tonight!

FRITZ: Now you see! He's Started and we're ready!

WANDA: There is Henry! But we haven't started!

DIRECTOR: I didn't tell him to start!

HENRY: I thought I was suppose to start!

FRITZ: Who told him to start the blasted thing? Who wanted to start before everyone was ready?

WANDA: Just go back and wait until we're ready!!

DIRECTOR: Are you accusing me of sending the stupid fool out here?

HENRY: I was ready! I don't think you should tell Me when to start and when to wait! You're not the director!

FRITZ: Did I say you did?!

DIRECTOR: You didn't have to! You implied it!

WANDA: I'm not telling you what to do! I'm telling you the show hasn't started yet!

FRITZ: Implied?! Ha! If you knew what you were doing, we wouldn't be in this mess!

HENRY: Don't raise your tone! I've done over 200 plays! I think I know when to start and when not to start!

DIRECTOR: Now I don't know what I'm doing huh? Listen, you untalented two-bit actor!

WANDA: But nobody Else is Ready to START Old Man!

FRITZ: Untalented?! You couldn't direct
your way out of a paper bag!

HENRY: That's it! I don't need to stand here and take this!!
(exits)

DIRECTOR: That's it! I don't need to stand
here and take this!! (*exits*)

WANDA: Well fine!! (*exits*)

FRITZ: Well fine!! (*suddenly realizing audience*) Oh!
Terribly sorry! This was not part of the.. performance as in
the script, you see, it was just a little..uh..you know..an
improvised exercise.. to..

DREW: (*enters quickly*) Dude! I'm sorry I'm late! (*looks at
crowd*) Oh snap! Have we started?

FRITZ: No! We haven't Started!!

DREW: Sweet! Check it out, I had to grab a cab and I'm a
little short of fundage, (*Cab driver/Host appears Stage
Right*) Could you give the cab dude some bucks? I gotta
go get ready! Thanks man!!

CAB DRIVER/HOST: (*looking around at audience etc*)
What's going here? You's guys havin' some kinda meetin'
up in here? Tupperwear? Amway? Playin' bingo?

FRITZ: (*irritated*) No, it's not a meetin'! Actually, it's a play.

CAB DRIVER/HOST: A play? Oh! One of them artsy fartsy deals. Like one of them "Romeo! Romeo! Who's the art without thou?" One them kinda deals?

FRITZ: Yes. Methinks so.

CAB DRIVER/HOST: "But soft, who broke the light bulb through yonder window'"?

FRITZ: You know, you're quite good actually. You have a real flair for the stage!

CAB DRIVER/HOST: Really? You ain't just saying that are you? You ain't trying to sweet talk me outta the cab fare? Cause it's five forty-two. (*holding out hand*)

FRITZ: That wouldn't be fair would it? My dear cab person, I will be most delighted to get your money if you could do me one small favor? One minuscule thing while I fetch your fare.

CAB DRIVER/HOST: Depends on what it is. I don't have to move anything heavy do I? Like a fridgerator or a steamer trunk full of romance novels and broken cinder blocks.

FRITZ: A what? A steamer trunk full of...? No! No! I simply need someone to take over for a moment and read this information to the audience. And since I was so impressed with your acting ability, I believe you would be the perfect person to handle the job. (*hands cab driver rules*)

CAB DRIVER/HOST: You want me to read this, to them?

FRITZ: Yes. And I will go post-haste and get your Five forty two. (*exiting -saying the following very quickly:*) Thank

8

you ever so much! You are most kind. You have a real star quality, I'm not just saying that, I'm most sincere. Thank again. Bye! (*exits*)

(*Cab Driver will read info -see appendix - when completed cab driver exits and Muffy and Blake stroll on. They stand for a moment as if waiting. Blake clears throat loudly. All of the following should be overdone, melodramatic, and very bad*)

HENRY: (*from off stage*) Don't tell me when to start! I know when it's time to start! (*enters*) Night has fallen upon the day! The branches sing from the mighty larks that are on the trees from the oaks that are on...the ground. Outside. What a delightful affair Mr. Wansillow...uh Sillwallow..is having this evening! Look! For it is the two young lovebirds! Good evening to you young bird.. loves!

BLAKE: Good evening Mr. Druthers.

MUFFY: Isn't the evening, ever so delightful!

HENRY: Yes! Tis! Tis indeed! It's just..uh.. and I...shall I uh..(*digs out script*)

BLAKE: I believe you were going to GO?!

HENRY: (*consulting script*) Just a second! I don't know where the..(*reading*)..blasted thing...

MUFFY: Why yes, Mr. Druthers! You were going to GO and *See How the Dinner was coming along*, weren't you?

HENRY: Ah! Here we are! (*reading*) I will go and see how the dinner is coming along! (*puts script in pocket but remains on stage*)

9

BLAKE: Well? (*nods to indicate exit*)

HENRY: (*catching on*) Oh! Yes! (*exits*)

MUFFY: Oh darling! What a splendid party my dear uncle Swanwallow is having on this eve!

BLAKE: Yes, Melody! The sun has just rested its golden rays behind the distant fair blue horizon. The evening brings its crispness to the air!

MUFFY: Skippy darling, just imagine! You and I shall be married soon and we shall live in this glorious late Victorian house! We shall be ever-so happy and overwhelmingly enchanted! We will frolic night and day.

BLAKE: Let us not throw caution to the wind, Melody! I have noticed that Mr. Praetorian is in attendance at this evening's gathering!

MUFFY: You mean the *evil* Mr. Praetorian?! The man who plans to cheat my dear wealthy Uncle Swanwallow out of his fortune, including this house?

BLAKE: Yes! The very man! Should your Uncle fail on his latest business affairs, he will be forced to give the evil Mr. Praetorian this house as payment! If that should happen, we will be forced to live in my mother's basement in...dare I say? (*your community, city*)!

MUFFY: Oh! Le Horror! Le Horror!

BLAKE: Don't you fret your pretty little face Melody! I shall see that no evil comes to your Uncle! I swear by the love that burns... where ever it is, that loves burns, that we shall be happy!!

MUFFY: Oh Skippy! I shan't believe we won't be happy! I must go now. I must run to the nearest room, slam the door, throw myself across the bed and weep profusely for twenty minutes! (*she exits dramatically*)

BLAKE: Melody, wait! I'll weep with you! (*as he is about to exit*, Wanda *appears in doorway blocking his way*)

WANDA: Well, well, well! Skippy Storm! Fancy meeting you here!

BLAKE: (*backing away*) Sally Sinlace!

WANDA: Bet you didn't think you'd see me again! Leaving me on the French Riviera with only a toothbrush.

BLAKE: I didn't "leave" you Sally! I..I had to go get more.. funds for our..fun. The fun we were having needed funds.

WANDA: And I suppose your sudden engagement to Melody Melotone was your way of getting more funds?

BLAKE: Of course not! Melody and I are in Love!

WANDA: Love? Lord above! Now you're trying to trick me with love?

HENRY: (*enters and approaches an audience member*) I say! Sir Skippy! Come quickly! Young Melody has fallen under...(*realizes error, crosses to Blake*) I say! Sir Skippy! Young Melody has spellin under the fall.. uh felling under the spall...under the spell of the evil Mr. Praetorian!

BLAKE: What? My Melody has fallen under Praetorian?! Why, I'll give that no good deviate such a thrashing!

HENRY: They've gone upstairs to the uh..to his..(*digs out script*) Oh! What is that stupid line? Let's see, gone up to, gone up to, ah! Here it is! Gone up to *his room*! She appeared to be weeping. Walk to the left. Oh. (*puts script away and walks to the left*)

BLAKE: I must go to my Melody! I'll teach that n'er do well such a lesson! (*exits*)

(*Fritz enters with Dolores*)

FRITZ: Oh Lady Vanderventer, your beauty brings magic to my home! More magic than any soft cloud placed by an angel upon a delicate breeze.

DOLORES: Oh Mr. Swanwallow, you are ever-so kind and profoundly poetic.

FRITZ: Pish posh! It is not out of kindness that I recognize your beauty, but out of truth!

DOLORES: How you do go on! I can feel a flush rising to my cheeks!

(*Drew enters still tucking in his shirt*)

DREW: Mr. Swanwallow! Mr. Swanwallow! Skippy Storm is upstairs pounding very violently upon a door. He says he's going to inflict great bodily harm upon someone!

FRITZ: Good..

DREW: Good heavens! I must go and see! Perhaps I can..

FRITZ: Drew! (*breaking character*) That's my line! You're saying my line!

DREW: What? It is? Oh Snap! Why did I memorize it?

FRITZ: I don't know. Why is there air? (*beat -back in character*) Good heavens! I must go and see! Perhaps I can bring peace and an agreeable solution to this disturbance.

DOLORES: Oh sir! How you do go on!

FRITZ: Yes! I do! I must go on now and cease the madness! (*exits and* Dolores *follows*)

(Drew *crosses to* Wanda. *He has to awkwardly move* Henry *out of the way.*)

DREW: Well Sally, alone at last! (*looks at* Henry *and nods to indicate exit*)

HENRY: Oh! Right! (*exits -muttering*) I keep forgetting ...

WANDA: Yes! Alone at last!

DREW: Have all the plans been arranged?

WANDA: Don't worry Scooter, the plans are in motion as we speak.

DREW: Gee that's swell! If we pull this off, Melody will be mine, Skippy will be yours and Swanwallow's fortune will be ours!

WANDA: Let's not get our cups too full of confidence, Praetorian has to complete his part of the plot.

13

DREW: Of course! As soon as Praetorian scams Swanwallow out of his millions, everything will be complete!

WANDA: Ah! I hear someone coming! Quickly, let's go to a secret place and discuss our crimes further! (*they exit*)

(there is a slight pause as nothing happens - Wanda stomps back out)

WANDA: (*loudly*) Ah! I hear someone coming! Quickly, let's go to a secret place and discuss our crimes further!

(Fritz *and* Dolores *enter quickly -Wanda exits*)

FRITZ: It reminded me of the time I was in the jungle, the very heart of the darkness with Captain Willard. I held a ferocious tiger at bay with my electric razor! Just as I was ready to subdue the beast, a giant titzi fly buzzed the nape of my neck!

DOLORES: Oh dear! You are incredibly brave!

FRITZ: Why it's nothing Lady Vanderventer!

DOLORES: I thought for sure Skippy would choke the very life out of Mr. Praetorian!

FRITZ: Oh. Yes, that. (*to himself*) I should have let him!

DOLORES: I'm sorry?

FRITZ: What? Oh, "Shoo-da-le-deim". It's an East Borneo phrase I picked up in South Hampton. It means, "I'm glad I stopped him!".

DOLORES: Oh. Well, do go on Mr. Swanwallow, what happened after the teeny fly buzzed you?

FRITZ: "Teet-zee" fly!

DOLORES: Teetzee, teeny, they're all tiny!

FRITZ: Uh yes, anyway, I took the lace from my boot, still holding the tiger off with this hand.. (*awkward pause he looks offstage*) And I uh.. (*clears throat*) I..I ..I thought I heard Mr. Druthers coming!

DOLORES: Why yes! He SHOULD be COMING in any minute now!

(*They pause for an uncomfortable moment and then*)

FRITZ: You mean MR. DRUTHERS? COMING IN HERE?

DOLORES: YES! HE SHOULD BE. COMING IN HERE.

(*another short awkward pause*)

FRITZ: ANY MINUTE NOW! QUITE TRUE! MR. DRUTHERS WILL ENTER. I feel. It's well past time.

DOLORES: So, umm.. well, Fritz! Uh..Mr. Swanwallow.. anyway..

FRITZ: Yes? Miss...Lady Vanderventer..

DOLORES: Why don't we... why don't *you* continue with your story until Mr Druthers he gets in here?

FRITZ: (*nervously*) My story?

DOLORES: Yes! Why don't you *go on*.. you know, with your STORY. The story you were telling me.. You know, tell me about the.. the teeny tiny thing. Until, you know...

FRITZ: Oh yes! Sure. That! My story. Uh..well, the teenie..uh, Titzi fly flew down and..(*pauses and begins motioning madly to someone off stage*)

DOLORES: Yes? Go on, he flew down.. and?

FRITZ: Yes. He flew down and...picked up a uh...

DOLORES: ...picked up a...? What did he pick up?

FRITZ: Huh? Oh, picked up a large...uh.. steamer trunk full of romance novels and broken cinder blocks.

DOLORES: He did what?

FRITZ: He uh... picked up the... uh.. You know, perhaps I should go and get Mr. Druthers! (*starts to exit*)

DOLORES: (*stops him*) Oh no! (*slight pause*) I'll go! (*exits quickly*)

(Fritz *ad libs a few reactions; "wait!' etc. perhaps ad lib a few moments with audience, then crosses to a spot near the exit.*)

FRITZ: (*using hand to cover mouth -using different voice*) Mr. Swanwallow?! (*looks off stage as if Henry spoke*) Oh! Mr. Druthers! There you are! (*puts up hand - in voice*) Mr. Swanwallow, the cook wishes to see you in the kitchen! (*takes hand down*) Oh! Does she? Well! I'd better go and see at once! (*starts to exit*)

HENRY: (*entering*) Mr. Swanwallow?

FRITZ: (*stops*) Mr. Druthers!

HENRY: The cook wishes to see you in the kitchen.

FRITZ: Oh, does she? Well, I'd better go and see at once. (*exits*)

        (Muffy *enters with* Drew)

MUFFY: Leave me alone Scooter! You know I...(*seeing* Henry) Oh! Mr. Druthers! Aren't you supposed to be..? (*nods toward exit*)

HENRY: Oh! Yes! (*he exits -muttering*) Always telling me where I'm supposed to be! Enter here, exit there!

   (*MUFFY walks back to about where she entered and starts the scene again*)

MUFFY: Leave me alone Scooter, you know I love only, Skippy!

DREW: But there must have been a time when you felt something for me! Like that time I was in the joint. You would send me letters and cartons of cigarettes.

MUFFY: You weren't in the "joint" Scooter! It was a minimum security Halfway house for White collar criminals!

DREW: But still, it was dire! All those hardened criminals forcing me to caddy those their golf games! I should say my darling, your sweet letters were the only thing that got me through those long nights!

MUFFY: But that was *Then* Scooter! This is.... not then, anymore. Things have changed!

DREW: Oh have they? (*moves close to her*) Let's see how much change there has been! (*he takes her in his arms*)

(Wanda *and* Blake *enter, arm in arm*)

WANDA: ...and I still have the scuba gear.

BLAKE: Well, I still have the.. (*seeing them*) Melody!!

MUFFY: (*pulling away*) Skippy!!

BLAKE: (*shocked*) Scooter?!

MUFFY: (*shocked*) Sally?!

DREW: Skippy!

WANDA: Melody!

BLAKE: (*angry*) Scooter!!

DREW: Skippy?

MUFFY: (*angry*) Sally!!

WANDA: Melody?

(*Depending upon your productions set up with exits etc.. You may adapt this to best suit your venue. Originally this was a circular chase scene with Blake running at Drew chasing him off while Muffy runs at Wanda, chasing her out. Each pair will re-enter running opposite ways. They should circle a few times until stopping, off stage.* Cab

Driver/Host *wanders out ad libbing a few moments with audience i.e. where did Fritz go? Where's the money? And Exits a few moments of silence and then two gunshots and a scream will be heard.)*

HENRY: (*running on*) Good Lord! Mr. Swanwillow has been poisoned!! Somebody do something! Uh..uh..(*pulls out script*) ..Oh! Call an ambulance!!

FRITZ: (*enters*) Henry!! Henry stop!!

HENRY: Mr. Swanwallow is dead he...(*seeing* Fritz) Wait a second! You shouldn't be out here! You're supposed to be dead!

FRITZ: Ladies and gentlemen! I'm afraid there's been a tragedy!!

HENRY: (*consulting script*) I'm quite certain this is not right!

FRITZ: Our director... has been killed! Shot!

DREW: (*entering*) Hey! Who's the stiff out there?

FRITZ: The Director!! Now, please! Somebody do something! Call an ambulance!

HENRY: I've already done that bit! (*shows* Fritz *place in script*) See?

FRITZ: No Henry!! This is REAL!! Drew, call the police!! (Drew *exits*) This is terrible! Oh the Humanities!!

(Mamet *rises from audience.*)

MAMET: Pardon me, excuse me. *etc..*

FRITZ: Oh good!! Are you a doctor sir? Please, right this way! (*leads* Mamet *to exit*) Right out here! You see? It's awful. (Mamet *exits*) I'm sorry ladies and gentlemen, I'm not sure I can continue!

HENRY: Me either because I'm really lost! (*flipping through script*) I don't see any of this in here anywhere!

FRITZ: This really is a cute little play. Albeit rather contrived, amateurish and poorly written. Of all the Murder Mysteries I've done, this is surely...*one* of them. The director was such a dear friend. Of course, she had a temper and demanded too much of the actors. A tyrant and megalomaniac, but I say that with all due respect. I..I really don't know what we should do now!

HENRY: Well, for one thing, you're supposed to be dead! And then I come on and say you were poisoned. See? (*shows script*) It's right here! And then, from out of nowhere, a policeman arrives! He walks out here and says; "Everyone remain calm. Everything is under control!".

MAMET: (*enters*) Everyone remain calm. Everything is under control! Could I have all the actors in here please?!

FRITZ: Is the director...is she all right?

MAMET: I'm afraid a slug in the head has a capacity to leave you less than "All right". (*shouts the following in the direction of off-stage*) Johnson! Rico! I want the body outlined and everything dusted for prints! Call HQ and tell 'em our situation! Get forensics on the ball with this! Oh yea, most important! Save me a couple of those Glazed numbers and Long Johns! The ones with the custard not the nasty cream filled jobs. We're gunna be here awhile!

FRITZ: Excuse me, may I ask who you are? And who are those people out there?

MAMET: Detective Mamet. Special agent with the Alcohol Theater and Firearms division. (*flashes badge*) Those people out there are undercover agents.

FRITZ: Undercover agents?

MAMET: You got it pal! We've been stakin' out your audience because we were afraid somethin' like this would happen. Now, be a sport and get all your people of the theatrical persuasion in here for me. Thanks!

FRITZ: But..but..

MAMET: Just do it Mac! I gotta be sure none of the actors make the Big Exit, O.K.? Oh, see if the kitchen back there can brew up a pot of Joe for me, will ya? Thanks.

(Fritz *exits*)

MAMET: Sorry ladies and gents, but I'll need you all to linger a bit longer. We got a serious situation here. There's a million stories in the naked (*city/county*) and this..

HENRY: What page are you on?

MAMET: Page? I ain't on no page, pops! We're on the Big stage now! The real deal. The curtain's down and the Fat lady sang. You got me? A coupla gunshots grinded this show to a halt like a eighteen-wheeler at a twenty-four hour truck stop. You comprende? You capice?

HENRY: No, I'm Henry. Who are you supposed to be?

(Cast *begins entering during following. At some point* Henry *slips out.*)

MAMET: Detective Joe Mamet. (*beat*) It was a dark and rainy evening in the (*unincorporated/corporate suburb/city by the river/lake or whatever fits your locale*). The chief came into my office. I could see by his eyes, he was worried, uneasy, concerned. He handed a piece of paper, a report. The document sang to me its tune of trouble. It appeared we had some Crazed actor, a real oddball, a loose cannon who walked into theaters drippin' trouble liked they just stepped out of a bathtub full of mayhem. It seemed that "Murder Mysteries" were their specialty. They got their kicks, their jollies by making the plots of these plays, shall we say.."realistic"!

DOLORES: Oh dear! I've heard about this!

WANDA: Yea! I did "Murder at the Mansion" last fall! The lead actor was stabbed with an eyebrow pencil!

MAMET: And YOU were the Make-up person on the show, weren't you Miss Wanda Hawthorne?! In fact, all of you are connected to other groups that had similar incidents! (*gets out notebook and consults*) Fritz Fontaine; "Murder at Midnight". Actress was smothered with her costume! Dolores Dumpfy; "Murder at Noon". Producer was strangled with his stopwatch cord! Blake Powers and Muffy Ladue, you both were in "Murder in the Mall". The prop person was force fed her check-list!

BLAKE: So, what's your point?

DOLORES: Oh dear! Do you believe that one of us is...?

22

MAMET: Yes! The *Murder Mystery Murderer*!

EVERYONE: No way! Get out of here! *etc..*

MAMET: I've done my homework people! I had a hunch the trail would lead here! All of the facts and leads pointed to this play. This blessed plot, this earth, this realm, this theatre. And I was right! The killer is in this room!

EVERYONE: No way! Get out of here! *etc..*

MAMET: I knew this night would be like a tiger on rusty chain. The smell of murder hung in the air like a cheap cigar.

DREW: Dude! You sound just like this old movie I saw last night!

MAMET: It's Drew Graham right?

DREW: No, I think it was called "Detective Stone and the case of the Big Palooka"

MAMET: I meant your name, Drew Graham, Right?

DREW: Uh..wow! (*thinks for a second*) Yea!

MAMET: (*checking notebook*) It says here that you have a problem with bein' on time. Tonight was no different, was it Mr. Graham? (*to Fritz*) Mr. Fontaine, word on the street says your trip is your Ego. It's too big for someone proportionate to your height and weight.

WANDA: I'll say!!

MAMET: Miss Hawthorne, I hear your attitude is in need of a Tune up. It causes your mouth to shoot off when your brain is empty. (Muffy *and* Blake *snicker*) And Mr. Powers. Sources tell me your trouble is Dames. There's just so many and so little time. And then there's little Muffy Ladue. It says here your problem is everything! Especially people who like things you don't like.

MUFFY: Who said that! I don't like them!

BLAKE: How do you know all this?

WANDA: Yea! Who are these "sources"?

MAMET: My eyes and ears are like 'wallpaper' babe; they're all over this joint!

TRIXIE: (*entering with coffee cup*) Here you go Joey sweetie!

WANDA: Wait! That's our assistant Director!!

TRIXIE: Rico said to tell you there was no trace of gunpowder near the wounds, so it appears she was shot from a distance. It seems to be a .38 caliber slug. We've searched the premises but haven't turned up a weapon yet.

BLAKE: She's a COP?

TRIXIE: Surprise! Surprise!

BLAKE: I don't believe it!!

TRIXIE: Where did you think I got the handcuffs, sugar britches?

MUFFY: BLAKE!! (*slaps his arm*)

MAMET: Thanks doll. That'll be all for now. (Trixie *exits*)

WANDA: I always thought she was too a little too nosy!!

MAMET: all right, enough of the lolly-gagging, back to business! Let's get a handle on your locations at the time of the crime. The point of perpetration. You! (*to* Fritz) That was a nice little "scene" you had with the director earlier. You mind tellin' me where you were when she met their maker?

FRITZ: I uh..I was in the .... back. With.... Dolores. Isn't that right Dolores?

DOLORES: Huh?

FRITZ: You know, the story. Maybe you should finish with the story of where we were.

DOLORES: Oh! Yes! Story. We were.. up in the.. back..

MAMET: And what were you doin' in back?

FRITZ: We were...I was..tell him, Dolores!

DOLORES: Uh..we were..Fritz was..helping me..

FRITZ: I was helping her with her...uh..

DOLORES: With a.. steamer trunk full of romance novel and cinder blocks.

MAMET: With *a what*?

25

FRITZ: With her make-up! You see, that's just *theatre talk* for the application of stage make-up! Stage jargon.

BLAKE: It is?

MAMET: And where were you, Mr. Powers?

BLAKE: Who me? I was right here! You saw me! We were running around in that stupid chase scene!!

MAMET: And the murder happened right after the chase scene. So, where were you then? Near the director?

BLAKE: No. We were.. in the back. Not the back *they* were in. (*indicating Fritz and Dolores*) A different back. Way far away from the director.

MUFFY: (*somewhat whispered*) But they said the director was shot from a *distance*.

BLAKE: Distance? Oh uh..but not distantly far. Nearly.. far. Kind of.

MAMET: So all of you were...in the back?

WANDA: No. Drew and I weren't in the back.

MAMET: I see. And I don't suppose any of you, "heard" or "saw" anything?

DREW: Yea! We heard Blake and Muffy!

MAMET: You heard Blake and Muffy? You mean talking?

WANDA: I'm not so sure there was a lot of "talking" going on!

DREW: Just breathing. Like a lot of loud breathing.

BLAKE: Of course! We were out of breath from running around!

MUFFY: And my allergies and asthma are not helped by all the dust in here! (*she demonstrates breathing*)

MAMET: Yea, so, anyway! Let's see if I have all this straight now. Fritz and Dolores were in back. Blake and Muffy were in back..

BLAKE: But not much. Not at a *distance*.

MAMET: Right. Drew and Wanda were near. So that leaves Henry. And Henry was....wait! Where's Henry?!

FRITZ: Henry?! Henry!! I'll find him! (*exits*)

HENRY: (*enters from back*) Huh? What? Is it my line?

MAMET: Come here pal, I need to ask you some questions. I need to find out exactly where you were when the director was shot.

HENRY: Good Lord! The Director's been Shot?!

WANDA: Detective, Henry was off stage in the Foyer.

MUFFY: It's Foy-yeah! Not Foy-Yer!

WANDA: Oh! Pardon me! He was in the Foy-yeah!

MAMET: And how do you know this?

WANDA: I saw him. He was standing right out there. (*pointing offstage*) You see, he is supposed to come on right after our chase scene. He usually misses his cue, that's why I noticed he was actually where he was supposed to be.

MAMET: In the foyer.

WANDA: Foy-yeah.

MAMET: Foy-yeah. So, Henry. You were off stage?

HENRY: What? Oh! Am I suppose to be *off* stage? (*starts to exit*)

MAMET: (*stops him*) No! No! Henry, look pal! The play's over! You ain't suppose to be anywhere but right here, right now! Answerin' my questions! Your part is tellin' me if you saw anything when the director was killed.

HENRY: Good Lord! The director's been killed?!

MAMET: YES! The director is dead! Pushin' up daisies! Gave up the ghost! Shrugged off this mortal coil! Takin' a perpetual nap! The Big sleep! Bought the Farm! Filled out the form to take Harp lessons! (*looking into Henry's eyes*) Why am I even tryin'? It looks like the lights are on.

DOLORES: Detective, I'm afraid Henry is a little confused.

WANDA: Confused?! You mean Henry is a little drunk!

HENRY: Ohhhhh! I understand! This isn't the play!!

MAMET: Hello? I think someone came home!

HENRY: You want to know what happened before I ran in here and said; " Good Lord! Mr. Swanwallow's been poisoned!"

MAMET: Bingo! Exactly! What happened *before* that bit? When you were out in the Foyer..

MUFFY: Foy-Yeah!

MAMET: ..Foy-yeah. Did you hear anything? See anyone? Did you see the director?

HENRY: No. I saw Fritz..

MAMET: You saw Fritz?! (*looks for Fritz*) Now, where is Fritz?!!

DREW: Dude, I'll go get him! (*exits*)

HENRY: Yes, you see, I never quite know when I'm suppose to run out here and say; "Good Lord! Mr. Swanwallow has been poisoned!" So, Fritz usually stands nearby and signals me. He waves like this! (*demonstrates*) And when he signals, I know I'm suppose to run out here and say; "Good Lord! Mr. Swanwallow has been poisoned!" At least I think it was Fritz waving. Actually I can't see very well without my glasses.

FRITZ: (*entering*) I believe I can clear this up, detective.

MAMET: And where have you been?

FRITZ: Tidying up a few things. Your assistant Trixie can explain. Oh, Dolores, here is your lipstick, I believe you dropped it. (*hands it to her*) You see, detective, I usually stand nearby and signal Henry to enter. But tonight, after

29

my little discussion with the director,she felt it should be (his/her) job to direct the actors. Therefore, she was going to signal Henry. It was the *director* in which Henry saw, not I.

MAMET: And what's this info Trixie has? Is it something you can share with all of us?

FRITZ: For my safety and yours, I request you see her about the matter.

BLAKE: Look Mamet, this is really getting boring!

MAMET: Powers? Is that your trap I hear flappin' back there? You'd better stick a cork in it until I ask for your opinion!

BLAKE: What's your badge number? My father personally knows the Governor!

MAMET: Oh is that right? I suppose it was your dear daddy that got you cleared of suspicion charges in the last Murder Mystery case! Listen pal, your old man's influence don't wash nothin' around here. It's a rusty bucket, it don't hold water! Ya got me? I don't care who your daddy knows, you're a suspect like everyone else! Do I make myself clear??

BLAKE: I don't have to say anything without proper representation!

MUFFY: You tell him Blakey! You don't have to say anything to him! Besides, his diction is terrible!

WANDA: Here she's goes!

MUFFY: Excuse me? Do you have something to say to me?

WANDA: Yes, but not now. We're in mixed company.

BLAKE: That's it! You keep your mouth shut or else I'll...

(BLAKE and WANDA begin ad-lib arguing -overlapping with each other -until)

MAMET: Girls! Girls! Please! Enough with the fightin. Can we return to the business at hand? Thank you! Now, I need each of you to go out and show my men exactly where you were at the time of the murder. That back stage area is a central fixture in this joint. It's accessible from many locations. One can lean out a doorway and have a clear shot. Whether you're near, *(to Drew and Wanda)* or in the back, *(to Fritz and Dolores)* or in the back but not at a distance.*(to Blake and Muffy)* You all had opportunity. As far as motive, well, with psychos there never is a motive. Take out the motive, all you got is opportunity and locations. And you all had prime locations!

BLAKE: Ha! Not where Muffy and I were!

MUFFY: Blakey's right!! The broom closet is nowhere near the stairs!

MAMET: Broom closet?

BLAKE: Muffy!!

WANDA: He takes you there too, huh?

BLAKE: Wanda!!

31

MUFFY: Excuse me?

WANDA: Oh sorry! Did I say that out loud?

MAMET: May I ask, what you were doin' in the closet?

BLAKE: Closet? Oh yes, I uh..saw some.. dirt and...Muffy and I went to the closet to ...find a broom to sweep up the dirt I fondle..Found!!

WANDA: (sarcastic)Sure! Seems legit.

BLAKE: Well, it's true! We went into the closet and while we were in there, the banging started!

MAMET: Excuse Me?

BLAKE: The gunshots! The *banging* of the gunshots!

MAMET: And then what did you do?

BLAKE: I came out of the closet!

WANDA: I knew it was just a matter of time!

BLAKE: That does it! (*starts for Blake*)

WANDA: Go ahead Blakey! Come at me bro!(*starts for Blake*)

(Mamet *steps in-between them, holding them off. They continue to bicker -ad lib- which starts off a chain reaction of chaos.* Fritz *and* Dolores *begin arguing - perhaps over his alibi or something related.* Drew *and* Muffy *join in the banter with Wanda and Blake.*

*(Cont).*Henry *begins spouting lines - either from the play or some other play -i.e. Shakespeare monologue. It should be a cacophony with* Mamet *trying to maintain order above all the noise.)*

TRIXIE: *(enters -loud whistle if possible)* SHUT UP!! *(everyone does)*

MAMET: Thanks Trix, but I had the situation under control.

TRIXIE: *(holding up some papers)* Joey, I need to see you.

MAMET: All right, I was just about to send these mugs out anyway. O.K. everyone, listen up. I want you to go out and show the nice flat foots exactly where you were at the time of the shooting. Then, I'll need to see you all in your dressing rooms where you will happily agree to allow us to search your personal effects. I'm sure none of you will object.

FRITZ: But Detective!!

MAMET: Yes? You have some objection Mr. Fontaine?

FRITZ: No, not that. What about them? *(indicates the audience)*

MAMET: What about 'em? Plays have intermissions don't they? We'll just take a little intermission. *(if dessert is being served of just intermission adjust dialogue here.)*

DREW: *(entering)* Wow! Here you guys are! So, what going on? I guess we're not going to do the play now right?

WANDA: Seriously?!

MAMET: Seriously they came to see a Mystery right? I believe the M.O. with these plays is that they help solve the murder, right? So, instead of some fictional fancy made up murder, they can help solve a real murder. We got own real live Murder Mystery right here! Is that all right with you guys? (*invoke response)* Great! You see? Now, all of you. Chop-chop! Let's go!

(*Cast begins exiting*)

FRITZ: Mr. Mamet, I just wanted to say, the director was a dear friend of mine, Miss Trixie can attest to that. This sudden unnatural death affects me most of all and I just feel I should tell you...

WANDA: Fritz! The play's over! You can stop acting now!

FRITZ: Miss Hawthorne! I am merely doing my civic duty in assisting the law enforcement agents in every way I can!

WANDA: You've got a little brown stain on your nose there Fritz.

(Fritz *begins to wipe nose, realizes Wanda's implication, then exits with a huff*)

BLAKE: (*as he exits*) Come on Muffy! I going to call Father!

MUFFY: But I have to go to the bathroom!

BLAKE: Fine! You go winkle tinkle and I'll call father! (*they exit*)

(Henry *is only one remaining on stage.*)

MAMET: Henry, pal, you want to uh..(*nods toward exit*)

HENRY: Oh! Yes, of course! (*exits*)

MAMET: And I thought I was goin' to find one psycho in this group!! O.k. Trix, what'dya got for me?

TRIXIE: Couple of things. Here's the director's personal notes. There's some interesting information in there.

MAMET: Swell! Maybe they'll help me understand why she gathered a bunch like this!

TRIXIE: Made a few calls too. Since March of 2010, six theater groups have had homicides. As you know, every actor in this play was connected to those groups in some manner. Five of our suspects here tonight, were also suspects in the other plays!

MAMET: You mean five of these mugs were in every Mystery that had a murder?

TRIXIE: That's a big ten-four, Joey! (*consulting notebook*) Fritz Fontaine, Drew Graham, Blake Powers, Muffy Ladue, Henry Figgens and Wanda Hawthorne. But nothing was ever pinned on any of them. It's kinda funny they're all here tonight!

MAMET: So why would a director bring all these people together if their pasts were so shady, so dark, so wrapped in suspicion like a pastrami on rye, hold the mayo?

TRIXIE: Maybe it was the intention. Five suspects in one play..

MAMET: Yea, I get it Trix. Like puttin' a bunch of monkeys in a room full of typewriters, eventually one of 'em is gunna write the next great sitcom.

TRIXIE: I'm thinking that the director knew something.

MAMET: Maybe knew too much!Whatever it was, it's gone. The only thing on the director's mind right now is a . 38 slug.

TRIXIE: Oh! That reminds me! We found the gun!!

MAMET: You did?! Where was it?

TRIXIE: It was stashed back in a broom closet.

MAMET: Thanks toots! You've done good!

TRIXIE: Thanks Joey. It was my pleasure!

MAMET: All right everybody! We'll take a little break, smoke 'em if you got'em, but do so outside. We'll all meet back in here in (*15/20)* minutes. Keep your lids peeled for any clues. Remember everything you've heard so far. Trix and I will see you all in a little while. (*they exit* and Cab Driver/Host enters)

CAB DRIVER/HOST: O.K. Listen up you's guys. They wanted me to make announcement (*give whatever instructions etc.)*

END OF ACT I

Act II

(Fritz enters with Cab Driver/Host before everyone else- holding piece of paper)

CAB DRIVER/HOST: O.K. Now, if I do this I'll get my five forty two?

FRITZ: Yes. I promise.

CAB DRIVER/HOST: O.K. (*looking at paper*) Welcome back to the second half. We hope you enjoyed the.. whatever you had etc...etc   blah blah blah. Yadda yadda yadda. O.K. where's my money?

FRITZ: I believe Mr. Mamet has it for you. He's outside changing his oil.

CAB DRIVER/HOST: Yea? Well you better not be pullin' my chain buddy, cause if you are...you'll be sorry! (*exits*)

FRITZ: Hello again, ladies and gentlemen. May I say how sorry I am your evening was disrupted like this. Perhaps we can accommodate you all by giving you a discount rate on our summer musical. It's a delightful piece I have written myself. A musical adaptation of the play, The Miracle Worker. It's called, Sunday in the Dark with Helen.

TRIXIE: (*enters*) Oh! There you are! (*turns and calls out doorway*) Hey Joey! He's in here!

FRITZ: (*to audience*) The play we *were* doing this evening was indeed a delight. I actually had quite a dramatic death scene. As you may know, Mr. Swanwallow, whom I was portraying, ingested poison and dies. It was a brilliant scene. Here, allow me to demonstrate before everyone

37

else arrives. (*acts this out*) I come stumbling in on stage. I am clutching my throat and gasping for precious oxygen. I turn a few times and struggle to utter some prophetic final words. "Do not go gentle into that good night! Rage! Rage! Against the Machine! Uhhh! Aggg!

TRIXIE: Fontaine!? What are you doing?

FRITZ: Then I turn once and fall to center. (*lies down*) My hand reaches up, as if to welcome the oncoming void of death. I reach for the light. And alas, darkness. I die.

TRIXIE: You want to get up off the floor pal?

(*cast begins to enter*)

DREW: (*entering*) Dude! Is he dead now too?!

WANDA: (*entering*) Hey! I didn't know we had time to take a nap!

MUFFY: (*enters and screams*)!!

WANDA: Can I slap her?

TRIXIE: Come on! Get up Fontaine!

DOLORES: (*entering*) Oh Gosh! Has Mr Fontatine succombed to violence as well?

MAMET: (*entering*) What's going on in here?

TRIXIE: He was showing everyone his "death scene".

MAMET: I need to see his getting up off the floor, scene! Is everyone here? Who are we missing?

TRIXIE: Looks like we're missing...Blake and Henry. I'll go get 'em. (*she exits*)

MAMET: Thanks toots. Now, back to business. I got my mits on some interestin' info here. (*holds up papers*) The Directors notes! There's a lot of scribblin' in here about this and that, but when you add it up, one thing's clear! Your director took it upon (himself/herself) to play detective! Now I understand why she picked actors who were suspects in the other murders! That was the plan, the scheme, her kick, her dangerous and devious intention. she thought she could find the killer! But the killer found her first. They tumbled the game and helped her cross the big finish line! Do not go past go, do not collect 200 dollars.

BLAKE: (*entering*) All right ! All right! I'm going!

TRIXIE: (*entering*) Here he is! I found him in the back scarfin' down snacks! I haven't found Henry yet.

(*During the following dialogue, Blake should be pulling various snacks from his pocket and eating them.*)

FRITZ: Excuse me, I believe I know where he may be. May I go look?

MAMET: I don't know Fontaine. Havin' you people just wanderin' around ain't safe.

FRITZ: I did get awfully parched from my Death Scene. I could use a cool drink.

MAMET: Oh all right! Trix, you go with him. Don't let him outta your sight!

TRIXIE: Sure thing Joey. Come on Fontaine! (*they exit*)

39

MAMET: O.K. Now, where was I?

DREW: Uh..you were standing over there! (*pointing to a spot*)

MAMET: No, no! I mean, what was I sayin' before?

EVERYONE: (*starts repeating different parts of Mamet's previous speech about the director. It should be a jumbled.*)

MAMET: O.K.! O.K.! Yeah, yeah! The Director's notes! Now, the director had a gut feeling that one of you mugs was the *Murder Mystery* killer! We know that five of you were involved in plays that had a murder. That's why some of you were cast in this show. It seems the director had been studyin' each of you and narrowin' down the suspects. The vote was about to cast on the lead candidate. But the pollin' place got closed early. All we have to go on is this! (*holding up notes*) The last thing she scribbled in here was; "The killer is very intelligent. Very sly. And quite an actor. I believe I know who their target will be. Tonight I will know for sure. I will catch them in the act!" Well, the only act the director caught was the final one! The target was her! So, who did she think the psycho was? And who did she think the target was? I bettin' one of you knows more than you're lettin on! If you do, you'd better start singin'!

HENRY: (*entering in back -singing*) To Dream the impossible dream! To Fight the unbeatable foe...

WANDA: He's finally snapped!
MAMET: (*goes to get him*) All right, pal!

40

HENRY: (*as Mamet grabs him*) *Touch me, It's so easy to leave me. All alone in the moonlight..*

MAMET: Come with me Mac! (*pulls him up front*)

HENRY: *It's time to try defying gravity. I think I'll try defying..*

MAMET: Here Dolores. Keep some reins on him.

DOLORES: You keep still Henry. I don't want to have to hurt you.

MAMET: Great! Now I got show tunes in my head! O.K. Here's the deal! As most of you know, we found the murder weapon. The location in which it was found seems to implicate a particular person and/or persons in this room. But I'm sure it's not that easy. If this killer's as smart as the director thought, they may be tryin' to pin the goods on someone else! One of you may be a patsy.

BLAKE: A what?!

WANDA: He said Patsy, not Pansy!

BLAKE: Oh!

MAMET: Now, we're through the lookin' glass here people! Black is white. And white is black.

(Trixie *and* Fritz *enter. Fritz is holding a small cup.*)

TRIXIE: I see you found Henry. One of the caterers saw him coming out of the closet.
MAMET: The caterers? I never considered questioning the caterers.

41

TRIXIE: It's covered. I questioned the caterers and the cabbie.

MAMET: Questioned the cabbie?

TRIXIE: Cabbie and caterers are completely clear.

MAMET: Hmmm. Concerning this closet he came outta. The same closet where we confiscated the criminal configuration?

TRIXIE: Correct.

MAMET: Coincidence?

TRIXIE: Could be.

MAMET: Capable?

TRIXIE: Could we consider?

MAMET: Could.

TRIXIE: Considered it considered.

MAMET: Cool..

TRIXIE: Curiouser and curiouser

FRITZ: Could I say something? (*hands his cup to someone to hold - it should be passed around as no one wants to hold it for long.*) Henry is prone to take a drink every now and again. He keeps his "supply" in various hiding places.

MAMET: Let me guess, like a broom closet? This closet is a very popular place!

FRITZ: Actually, many of us use it. What I mean is; sometimes there isn't time to change costumes or fix your make-up, so we use the closet.

TRIXIE: He's right Joey. A lot of people use it.

MAMET: So, who used it tonight beside Blake, Muffy and Henry?

FRITZ: I'm not certain. Since the play was halted so early in the evening, not everyone had an opportunity to use its facility. That's why I suggested to Miss Trixie to look there first.

MAMET: What are you talkin' about Fontaine?

FRITZ: Didn't she tell you?

MAMET: Tell me what?

TRIXIE: It was Fritz's idea that we look in the broom closet for the murder weapon.

MAMET: Oh yea? Why were you so sure it would be there?

FRITZ: I wasn't. I just assumed it was a likely place. Immediately after the shots were fired, you and your lovely assistant Trixie were quick to take charge and gather everyone in here. Keeping that in mind, the killer had little opportunity to dispose of the weapon.

MAMET: So, you're sayin he or she chucked it the closet? A closet where everybody goes? And anyone could find it?

FRITZ: I doubt they considered that. It was perhaps an...impulsive or panicked decision.

MAMET: You got a lot of ideas Fontaine. How do you know so much?

FRITZ: Well, since I'm in the business of... uh being in a lot of Murder Mysteries. One acquires a knowledge of investigation and deductive reasoning.

HENRY: (*singing*) I am the very model of a modern Major-General, I've information vegetable, animal, and mineral,

MAMET: Keep that mug quiet, will ya? Look Trixie, I gotta go and check on some things. I need you to take over. (*to Fritz*) If I'm not mistaken, don't these gigs usually have a Q and A session?

FRITZ: Yes of course! A very popular feature.

MAMET: All right Trix, you're in charge. You handle the questions. I'll be right out there. If you need any help just whistle. You know how to whistle don't ya?

TRIXIE: I just put my lips together and blow.

MAMET: Yea. Uh..I'll..I'll be..right back. (*exits*)

TRIXIE: All right! It's question and answer time folks! Let's see, where should I start? How about..Blake and Muffy. Would you please step up here? Thank you. Now, you stated that at the time of the murder, you were in the broom closet. Did anyone actually see you go in there?

BLAKE: I don't know.

TRIXIE: So, after your scene in here, your "chase" scene, you went off stage, "saw some dirt" and went to the closet to get a broom. And while you were in the closet, looking for this "broom", you heard the shots. Is that correct?

MUFFY: Uhhhh..What was the question?

BLAKE: Yes! For the millionth time! We were in the closet when we heard the shots! No, we didn't see anything or anybody! We came out and everyone was running around.

TRIXIE: What about before that? During the play, when you were running around? Did you see anything? Like the director standing there?

BLAKE: I was running! I wasn't looking!

TRIXIE: But you were running right passed the director.

BLAKE: So? I'm a very focused actor! I don't let little things like someone getting shot distract me!

TRIXIE: What about you Muffy? Did you see the director? Or anyone near the director with a gun? Or anyone shooting the director?

MUFFY: What does that have to do with the murder?

WANDA*:* Can I slap her now?

BLAKE: Look! You're a cop and you were undercover, how come you didn't see anything? You were working with the director! How come you don't know anything?

TRIXIE: I was seated back there, during the show, keeping my eye on You people. And you're wrong Blakey boy! I do know a lot of things. Where do you think we got all our info? Huh? All the facts about You and the Wicked Witch from (*a particular affluent area*) there?

MUFFY: What?! Well, that just goes to show what you know! I'm from (*name of nearby wealthy community- i.e. a city or community within the affluent area*) Miss Smarty Pants!

TRIXIE: I stand corrected. Anyone? Care to question these two? (*field a few questions*) O.K. Now, Wanda and Drew, please step forward. You stated that at the time of the murder, you two were nearby the stage.

DREW: Yea! We went out and showed those dudes earlier.

TRIXIE: And you also stated that neither of you saw or heard anything, beside hearing Muffy breathing and seeing Henry in the foyer.

WANDA: Yes! Yes! We've been through this! Why don't you people write this stuff down!

TRIXIE: During intermission, while we were all the dressing rooms, you told Detective Mamet that you saw Henry for an instant, from the doorway, after that you walked away.

WANDA: Yes! What was I suppose to do? Stand there and stare at him?

TRIXIE: Where did you go when you "walked away"?

WANDA: What do mean, "where did I go?"

TRIXIE: I mean, didn't you tell Detective Mamet something about wanting to go to the restroom?

WANDA: Yes. I said I was going to go to the bathroom to touch up my lipstick but I never made it because somebody starting shooting.

TRIXIE: May I ask what color lipstick you have?

WANDA: It's red!

TRIXIE: May I see it?

WANDA: (*purses her lips as if she's about to kiss someone*) See?

TRIXIE: I mean the actual lipstick. In the container.

WANDA: I don't have it! You see, Muffy borrowed it right before the show! I'd forgotten that. So, you see, I would have gone to the bathroom for nothing.

MUFFY: Oh that reminds me Wanda, I lost your lipstick. I must have dropped it somewhere.

WANDA: Lost it?

MUFFY: Yes. I was going wipe off any bacteria or diseases you may have gotten all over it and when I went to get it, it was gone! Somebody probably stole it! That's who we should be trying to find! We should be finding the thief and not some stupid murderer!

TRIXIE: Well, our stupid murderer was clever enough to scribble a message on the bathroom mirror. It reads, "There are no small actors. Only dead directors." He or she managed to do this right under our noses!

WANDA: Well it couldn't have been me!

MUFFY: It couldn't be me either! The thief has it! That's probably who the Killer is! It's the lipstick thief! Do I have to figure out everything for you?!

TRIXIE: Thank you Muffy. Anybody have any questions for these two? (*take questions*) O.K. Next, Fritz and Dolores, step up. Now, you stated you were in the back. Fritz was helping you with your make-up. What exactly was he doing?

DOLORES: Doing? He was..Well, he had an idea about the lipstick and...

FRITZ: No, not *lipstick*. It was *your rouge*.

DOLORES: Uh...Right rouge! Yes, my rouge because..

FRITZ: Because the deep rustic red was just too dark for her face. She's more of an Autumn.. complexion wise..

DOLORES: Yes, Autumn..

FRITZ: I thought I would take the opportunity to offer my opinion.

TRIXIE: I see. So, after your last scene, you went off and you took the "opportunity" to play Max Factor make over. And then...what?

DOLORES: Well, then..I or he...Oh, what's it called?

FRITZ: Then she agreed that.. yes, it was a tad too dark, the rouge that is... and I went to find.. to get a.. lighter shade for her cheeks.

TRIXIE: You "Went" to get a lighter shade?

FRITZ: Yes. Correct.

TRIXIE: So, you two weren't "together" the whole time?

FRITZ: Huh? Oh, well, no. Not the *whole* time.

TRIXIE: And I'm sorry, where did say you went? To get this lighter rouge?

FRITZ: As I told you and Detective Mamet earlier, we don't always have time to run hither and yon, so we keep the Make-up kit...It's sometimes kept...but not all the time...it's in...the uh...

DOLORES: The broom closet!

TRIXIE: How did I know you were going to say that?

DREW: Freak me out! I did too! I knew she was going to say Broom closet! What a trip! That's like just too weird!

FRITZ: But I never made it! I was hardly out the door when the shots were fired.

TRIXIE: All right, audience? Care to question these two? *(take questions)* All right. There is one little thing that bothers me with your story Fritz. You maintain you were "hardly out the door" but as I recall, the instant the murder was committed, you were one of the first people to run out here. Now, are we to believe, you were in the back, heard the shots, and managed to run out here in two seconds?

WANDA: Maybe he beamed down!

DREW: Yea! "Scotty! One to beam on stage!" "I can't get no power sir! She's lit up like a Christmas tree now! The dilithium crystal containment field is at maximum! Warp engines are off line! It'll take an hour before..

TRIXIE: (*starts interrupting around "Warp engines"*) Drew! Drew! Shut up!

DREW: Oh. Sorry. Computer? End program! Go ahead.

TRIXIE: Well, Fritz? Care to tell us the real Story?! You weren't with Dolores at all were you!

(Fritz *clutches his throat and begins to re-enact his Death scene again.*)

TRIXIE: Knock it off Fontaine! You're not getting out of this one!

(Fritz *slumps to the ground*)

TRIXIE: Fontaine? Hey! (*goes to him and checks*) Oh great!

WANDA: Oh that's just typical!!

TRIXIE: Somebody get Joey in here Now! (*she checks the cup he had been holding. Smells it etc..*)

HENRY: Good lord! Mr. Swanwallow has been poisoned!

MAMET: (*enters*) What's goin' on in here?

TRIXIE: It's Fontaine. (*holds up cup*) Somebody got to him.

MAMET: Slipped him a Mickey huh? (*takes cup - inspects*)

DREW: Woah! This is like Deja vu!

TRIXIE: I'm still getting a pulse.

MAMET: I believe someone spiked his water. Which one of you was holding this cup for him?

EVERYONE: (*they all say the name of a different person and point..etc..*)

TRIXIE: I think he's coming around!

FRITZ: (*sitting up*) Goodness! I'm sorry! (*looking at Trixie*) Mother! How lovely you are! The cranberry sauce is clogging the toaster this year mother. Shall I call the insurance rep? Is the Thanksgiving parade ready to begin? I'll set the DVR! We can watch it later. I'm afraid I've eaten all the thermal insulation!

MAMET: Oh swell! He's been drugged!

FRITZ: (*getting up*) Father! (*to Mamet*) I've milked the chickens and fed the cows! Can mother and I go to the dance competition now? I've been practicing!

MAMET; All right, get him outta here! In fact, all of you, clear the area and wait till I call you!

51

FRITZ: But I don't want to watch football today! I want to dance! (*he begins leaping and doing various bad ballet steps all over.*)

MAMET: Come on everyone! Outta here! Help me Trix!

(*Yet another chaotic moment erupts: Blake and Muffy begin complaining i.e. how long this is taking etc. Henry begins singing another Show tune. Dolores is trying to catch Fritz as he leaps about, along with Mamet. Trixie is trying to get everyone out -Wanda argues with her about questioning -i.e. You're not going to ask me this stuff again are you etc. Drew is delighted with Fritz and encourages him on, perhaps supplying music. Finally Mamet and Trixie usher everyone out. The stage is bare for a few beats: and Trixie and Mamet re-enter.*)

TRIXIE: Well, they should be all right. Rico and Johnson will keep their eyes on them.

MAMET: What do ya think Trix, any ideas so far?

TRIXIE: A few. You know, the entire time I was undercover as assistant director, none of them seemed very suspicious. But now!

MAMET: Well, they're actors Trix! You can't trust 'em as far as you could throw 'em.

TRIXIE: Fritz is a pompous wind bag. Dolores is quiet in a creepy way. Drew is a member of the Teen Age Wasteland. Muffy's a shinning dim bulb at the debutante ball. Blake's a wealthy snot nose 'player' and Henry's a confused old geezer.

MAMET: That's how they may seem! It's their cover, their ruse, their role. One of them is a cold blooded killer.

TRIXIE: But which one? Who could have shot the director, planted the gun in the closet and wrote the message in the bathroom with no one seeing?

MAMET: From what we know, anyone of them could have fired the fatal shots. But only a few were had the opportunity to wander free afterwords.

TRIXIE: Fritz! It was Fritz! He wandered around when he went to look for Henry!

MAMET: But why would Fritz drug himself?

TRIXIE: To throw us off and..and...Yea you're right. (*beat as she thinks*) Drew! Drew went to look for Fritz, while Fritz was looking for Henry! It was Drew!!

MAMET: The director said the killer was very smart and a very good Actor! I'm not sure Drew fits the profile. He's a few fries short of a happy meal.

TRIXIE: Yes but but.... So, who else was missing when we were all in here? (*beat*) Blake! It was Blake! He was gone for quite a while! Plus there's the closet connection!

MAMET: Of course, we have the issue of Wanda's missing lipstick. It matches the color of writing on the mirror! Kinda funny she "conveniently" lost it.

TRIXIE: Muffy! She lent it to Muffy! Muffy lost it! And Muffy had to go to the bathroom, right as we all left! And she was in the closet too!

53

MAMET: Yes, but don't forget, Muffy and Wanda aren't the only broads that were lipstick.

TRIXIE: But I don't wear that shade Joey! I don't..

MAMET: No, no! Not you Toots!

TRIXIE: Dolores! She wears red! And she is awfully quiet. You know, it always turn out to be the really quiet ones!

MAMET: It looks like suspicion could shine its cold light on any of these characters. But I got a feeling I know who the main perpetrator is!

TRIXIE: Who Joey?

MAMET: Well, I did some checking while you were questioning the suspects.

TRIXIE: And?

(Cab Driver/Host *enters*)

CAB DRIVER/HOST: And neither one of you have a clue do ya? It very obvious if ya ask me!

TRIXIE: Oh yea?

CAB DRIVER/HOST: Yea! Look I ain't no cop but I got this one nailed. I've had time to snoop around while waiting for somebody to come up with my dough. I've heard and seen everything since the start. I had the answer just like that! It's easy!

TRIXIE: Oh yea? Well, who is it?

CAB DRIVER/HOST: I said "it's easy" I didn't say "I'm Easy". Maybe somebody comes up with some overdue paper, cabbage, scratch, maybe I'll do some talkin'.

TRIXIE: Well, maybe we already know who did it.

CAB DRIVER/HOST: Maybe a lot of people know who did it!

MAMET: Well why don't we find out?

CAB DRIVER/HOST: Yea! Why don't we?

TRIXIE: Well I'd like to know your theory before we find out everyone else's. If that's ok?

CAB DRIVER/HOST: Go ahead Joey. I'll handle this part.

MAMET: 10-4 (*Trixie and Mamet exit*)

CAB DRIVER/HOST: Ladies and Gents, Now is the time of the evening when you cast your vote. In your folder you will find a piece of paper to write down the name of the person or persons you feel are the murderer. (*adapt this to whatever method is best..i.e having someone collect them. When completed the Cab Driver/Host will exit*)

(Mamet *and* Trixie *reenter*)

MAMET: All right, may I have all the actors back in here?

(*Cast begins to enter. Fritz leaps through doorway but Trixie settles him down.*)

DOLORES: Mr. Mamet sir? I'm afraid that Mr. Figgens is somewhat.. asleep on the floor.

MAMET: Oh brother! (*shouting out doorway*) Johnson? Rico? Do you mind haulin' Henry in here for me? Thanks!

MUFFY: Do we really have to have Henry in here? I think it's disgusting. This whole evening "stinks" enough!

WANDA: It only stinks when you're acting Muffy!

MUFFY: Oh very funny Wanda!

(*Henry is brought in - semi walking and placed on a chair*)

EVERYONE: (*Can ad-lib various chatter to cover Henry's entrance.*)

MAMET: O.K. Is everyone here? Good. Let's get it started in here. Trix, would you like to begin?

TRIXIE: Why thank you Joey. All right, listen up! Detective Mamet and I had a little talk a few minutes ago. We went over the evidence and the clues. We believe we know who the killer is!

BLAKE: Well, it's about time!
TRIXIE: Yes, isn't Blake? You may or may not know, we found the murder weapon in your love closet. You and Muffy were the only people who were linked to the closet around the time of the murder.

MUFFY: So? What's your point? (*Muffy digs out breath spray from hand bag*)

TRIXIE: The point is, Drew said he heard "breathing". Muffy was the one with the supposed "allergy attack". It was you he heard breathing so loudly, as you were so kind to demonstrate earlier!

MUFFY: So I was breathing! So, he heard me! So, that means I wasn't the killer! *(uses breath spray)*

TRIXIE: No, you weren't. Perhaps you were covering for someone. Someone who said he was with you.

BLAKE: I was with her! I've got the scratches to prove it!

TRIXIE: I'm sure you do.

BLAKE: I mean scratches from bumping into things in there. It's a small space.

WANDA: I guess that's how you got the lipstick on your collar? Bumping into Muffy?

MAMET: Nice shot there Wanda! But I'm sure you know something about lipstick traces, don't you? Or wasn't it *you* the director found in the same closet with Mr. Powers right before the show?

BLAKE: Who told you!?

MUFFY: Blake!! *(slaps his arm)*

MAMET: And didn't you tell the director that if anyone found out, she'd be sorry!

WANDA: So, you think I would kill somebody just because she found me and Blake rehearsing our kissing scene? Get a clue Mamet! I'm a method actress! I had to play

Blake's mistress in the stupid show, I wouldn't make out with him because I really wanted to!

MAMET: Oh! Just rehearsing huh?

WANDA: Yes. It was research.

TRIXIE: Such dedication Wanda! You're certainly a good actress.

BLAKE: I'll say!

MUFFY: BLAKE!! *(sprays him with breath spray)*

TRIXIE: So, we can eliminate Blake, Muffy and Wanda. *(perhaps she can do an aside to anyone in audience who picked them.)* How about Drew?

DREW: Oh no way man! I didn't kill anybody! I don't even eat meat!

TRIXIE: You were hanging out in the area of the director the entire time huh?

DREW: For sure Sir, Uh..dude, Ma'am.

TRIXIE: What about when you went to look for Fritz, when Fritz was looking for Henry?
DREW: I didn't find him.

TRIXIE: What took you so long to return?

DREW: It's a big place! I got lost.

TRIXIE: "Got lost"? "Lost" hiding a gun in the closet? "Lost" writing a message on the bathroom mirror?

DREW: No. Lost as in..*lost*. Like lost, because I was..you know, lost.

MAMET: His story checks out, Trix. He really was lost.

TRIXIE: I'm sorry, you lost me?

MAMET: I checked with Rico and Johnson. They found him lost.

BLAKE: Why don't you cut to the chase Mamet? If you know who the killer is, why all this boring exposition?

MAMET: Good point, Powers! But there's one thing you should all know. A little tid-bit I recently learned. Someone in this room is not who they seem. I just got word from HQ a while ago that one of you has beaten me to the punch. One of you has been on this case from the start. One of you is actually undercover detective Sam Saturday. You've been keepin' up quite a front to fool everybody. Detective Saturday also knows who the killer is! He had it cinched at the start of the night. In fact, the killer knew who he was as well. Yea, the killer tried to silence him several times this evening. Isn't that right Fritz Fontaine?!

TRIXIE: Fritz is the killer?!

MAMET: No, Fritz is Sam Saturday!

FRITZ: You found me out, huh? Well, lucky thing for me that narcotic didn't take full effect!

MAMET: You were the target the director spoke of in her notes weren't you?

FRITZ: That's correct. I was suppose to be in the same spot the director occupied this evening. I was the intended victim. But, I had to play along with the director so my cover wouldn't be blown. I had a feeling the killer would strike at that moment, but I was too late. I ran from the back and got there just as the director was being shot.

TRIXIE: So that's how you got out here so quick!

FRITZ: Dolores was kind enough to play along with my alibi. In fact, she and everyone else had no idea I wasn't Fritz Fontaine. I've been undercover since last fall. Pretending to be a pompous self centered creep, going from play to play, trying to get a handle on the Murder Mystery Murderer.

MAMET: Heck of an acting job pal!

FRITZ: Yes, but there's one more actor here tonight better than me!

MAMET: That's right! There's one person here who's been obvious from the get-go. But his "role" has lead everyone to believe he's incapable of murder. He's done everything but hit me over the head with his guilt. His killing of the director was more or less an accident. It was Fritz he was after! But it was a dark and gloomy night backstage. The shadow of the victim loomed in his vision. The silhouette danced in the killer's eyes. But the problem was...

TRIXIE: He couldn't see very well without his glasses!

(*Henry rises from couch quickly. He pulls a gun and grabs Muffy.*)

HENRY: That's right! You stupid fools! I'm the greatest actor of all time! But because of my age no one will cast me anymore! I get stuck in the kindly grandfather roles or the goofy absent minded uncle. I'm better than that I tell ya! I'm brilliant! I'm brilliant! I fooled everyone tonight, just like I fooled everyone for years. Playing the drunken old fool! But no one appreciated my talent! So they paid! They paid with their lives! I showed them! I showed them all how great I was! I've out acted everyone! No one suspected me ever!

WANDA: Well, he certainly fooled me!

DREW: For sure! Good job Henry!

FRITZ: Put down the gun Henry. Let the girl go.

HENRY: Oh no! This is the last season that I get passed over! There's a new year coming! No more goofy grandpas! I'm playing Lear! I'm playing straight dramatic roles! The classics! Maybe an occasional light hearted musical comedy. You can't stop me! You'll never take me alive coppers! You make one move and the little lady here gets it! Now, clear the way for my big exit!

MUFFY: (*irritated*) Seriously! Let go of me! Your breath stinks! Holy cow! (*sprays him in face with Breath spray*) Let go of me!
     HENRY jumps back trying to wipe face and eyes clear

MAMET: Quick! Somebody grab him!

   (*several people start for Henry but he breaks free and runs. Mamet, Trixie and Fritz take after him. This chase should be identical to the chase in the first act. As soon as all are off-stage two shots ring out. Mamet, Trixie and Fritz re-enter.)*

MAMET: You know Sam, you shoulda come clean with me earlier.

FRITZ: Well, I thought it best to play Fritz as long as I could. Sorry, Dolores.

DOLORES: Oh that's fine Fritz! I mean Sam. You kept me on my toes! I had to be..oh what's it called? (*pause*) Quick!

TRIXIE: So, let me see if I have all of this. Fritz was actually a cop who was pretending to be an actor. And he acted like this actor, so he could find the killer actor. And the killer actor was Henry. Who was really a killer but he was acting like he was an actor, but he really was an actor pretending to be a another actor but he was actually a killer.

WANDA: Just typical!

DREW: Man! What a trip!

MUFFY: Seriously? This was so Dumb!

BLAKE: This was as dumb as the real play!

MAMET: (*to Fritz*) He almost got you too! Lucky you didn't drink that water with the drug in it.

FRITZ: That's the problem. I did!

TRIXIE: You did?

FRITZ: It was only some mild hallucinogenic. It takes quite a while for it to really kick in.

(*Everyone looks at his or her watch.*)

FRITZ: You know, I really enjoyed acting these last few years. But you know what I really want to do now?

MAMET & TRIXIE: No, what?

FRITZ: I want to Dance! (*He leaps and dances down aisle*) I want to be free! I want to float like the beautiful wind! I am a bird flying through the sky .(*etc..till he exits*)

CAB DRIVER/HOST: (*enters*) All right! Who's got my five forty-two?

EVERYONE: (*follows after Fritz him ad-libbing various bits - Cab Driver/Host brings up rear still demanding money as they all exit.*)

THE END

APPENDIX

HOST - Rules of the game: *since some of the basic rules are covered in the dialogue, the Host need only read the following:*

1. Everything you see or hear from moment you arrive may be relevant to tonight's mystery.

2. Don't be afraid to share any clues with your neighbors. It may help to solve the mystery.

3. Please do not disturb the actors when they are acting. Some are very temperamental. You may talk back to your television at home, the actors on TV cannot hear you, the actors here tonight can.

4 (*Whatever else may be necessary*)

During the question and answer session.

- Note: During the section where Fritz is being questioned.
- Be prepared in case anyone picks up on Fritz's early entrance and puts the question to him. In that case proceed by eliminating Trixie's follow up question on the same matter.

CLUES

To be written on the restroom mirror before intermission: (*in Red Lipstick*) :
    "There are no small actors Only dead directors"

Hence- every female should wear the same shade of lipstick .

(If possible) prior to intermission: Where murder took place, have it roped off with Police Crime Scene tape and a white tape outline of a body.

 Little bits of paper - with handwritten poems to be placed all over.

A) Never had a scene to steal
Why not make the murder real?

B) If it's the falseness no one understands,
  Give the reality a great big hand!

C) Oh to act, perchance to dream!
  One here, is not who they seem

    D) When it comes to brain, Who truly lacks? Or
    should it be thus,   Who truly Acts?

Production Notes

One aspect that we had a lot of fun with is the idea of the "Fake" play versus the "Real" play. The play that the group of actors are trying to present is "Murder Me Always", until of course the director is killed.

In the original production we handed out Two sets of Programs. The first program contained the Character Names and what roles they were playing.
Example: Fritz Fontaine............. Mr. Swanswallow.

At intermission we handed out the Real programs.

We also enjoyed making the "fake" play as <u>Bad</u> as possible. Allowing the actors to break the rules of theatre, such as "upstaging" and "turning their backs" etc.. Of course, the acting in the "Fake" play was also very Bad. Very much over the Top with a lot of unnecessary broad gestures. Similar to "Silent Movie" acting on a stage. Of course, when the "fake" play stops, so does all the "bad" bits.

The stage setting can also reflect the cheapness of the fake play. Since the acting is amateurish, the set may also reflect this. A poorly designed drawing room would be appropriate.

Made in the USA
San Bernardino, CA
06 January 2016